GAME FACE

Pressure Point

by Rich Wallace
illustrated by Tim Heitz

Calico

An Imprint of Magic Wagon
abdopublishing.com

abdopublishing.com

Published by Magic Wagon, a division of ABDO, PO Box 398166, Minneapolis, Minnesota 55439. Copyright © 2016 by Abdo Consulting Group, Inc. International copyrights reserved in all countries. No part of this book may be reproduced in any form without written permission from the publisher. Calico™ is a trademark and logo of Magic Wagon.

Printed in the United States of America, North Mankato, Minnesota.
092015
012016

Written by Rich Wallace
Illustrated by Tim Heitz
Edited by Heidi M.D. Elston, Megan M. Gunderson & Bridget O'Brien
Designed by Laura Mitchell

Extra special thanks to our content consultant, Scott Lauinger!

Library of Congress Cataloging-in-Publication Data

Wallace, Rich, author.
  Pressure point / by Rich Wallace ; illustrated by Tim Heitz.
      pages cm. -- (Game face)
  Summary: Seventh-grader Torry is feeling pressure on the basketball court because he has to guard a player on the rival team who is bigger and older than he is.
  ISBN 978-1-62402-135-0
1. Basketball stories. 2. Self-confidence--Juvenile fiction. 3. Teamwork (Sports)--Juvenile fiction. 4. Middle schools--Juvenile fiction. [1. Basketball--Fiction. 2. Self-confidence--Fiction. 3. Teamwork (Sports)--Fiction. 4. Middle schools--Fiction. 5. Schools--Fiction.] I. Heitz, Tim, illustrator. II. Title.
  PZ7.W15877Pr 2016
  813.54--dc23
  [Fic]
                                  2015024882

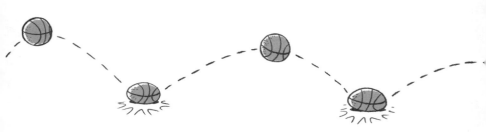

TABLE OF CONTENTS

ONE

Ice Cold

Relax, I told myself. *We've still got a chance.*

I took a quick glance at the scoreboard. We trailed, 43–38. Nineteen seconds remained.

It could still happen. A bucket, a steal, a buzzer-beating three-pointer. Overtime.

The inbounds pass smacked into my hands, and I sprinted up the court. Miles Robertson met me just past the midcourt line, forcing me wide. The Central point guard had frustrated me all night. But this game wasn't over yet.

Big Alan Mitchell rushed to the foul line and set a hard screen for me. I sliced past, but Robertson fought through. The guy is impossible to shake.

I drove toward the hoop. I could hear the crowd yelling.

Use that backboard, I thought as I lofted the ball in a high arc.

Not high enough. Robertson leaped and stretched.

Thwack!

I winced as the ball flew upcourt. Robertson had blocked the shot. Central was already on a fast break. I watched in frustration as the score turned to 45–38.

The final buzzer went off seconds later. I hadn't even moved.

"Nice game, Santana," Robertson said, sticking out his hand. I shook it weakly. Robertson ran off to join his celebrating teammates.

I walked off slowly.

Coach Mancini's postgame talk was a blur. I just stared at my locker. The sweat on my back turned ice cold.

"We'll get back on track tomorrow. Be on the court, ready to roll, at three fifteen," Coach ended.

I peeled my sweat-soaked BETHUNE jersey over my head and untied my sneakers.

I was wiped out. Guarding Robertson had drained every ounce of energy.

A poke to the arm made me look up. Marcus was next to me on the bench. He leaned in.

"Ouch," Marcus said softly. "You got schooled out there, Torry."

I tried to scowl at him, but I couldn't keep from breaking into a smile instead. Marcus always finds a way to make me laugh, even when I'm down.

"Robertson is good," Marcus said. "He made all the difference tonight."

Just what I wanted to hear. I covered Robertson the whole game. I was responsible for all of his points, those assists, those steals. And that last-minute block. That was all on me.

Marcus took off his orange jersey with the blue number 5 and folded it neatly. "Clean and dry," he said with a smirk. "All set for the next game."

"You've still got your goggles on," I said. "You didn't even play."

"I *look* like I played," Marcus replied. He took off the sports goggles and put on his regular glasses, then changed out of his huge sneakers. Marcus has big feet, even though he's my height. When he grows into those feet he'll tower over me.

Just four of us seventh graders made the Bethune Middle School Badgers. I'm the only starter, and the only one who played tonight. After a five-win start to the season, we'd expected to keep the momentum going before a packed house at home. But Central had clearly been the better team.

"Did you see the stat sheet?" Marcus asked. "Robertson had twenty-one points."

I kicked off my sneakers. I didn't need to see the statistics. I knew how many points I'd scored. Same number as my jersey: 3. All on free throws. Worst game of my life.

One of the eighth graders put on music. I liked the steady beat, but I was in no mood to enjoy it.

Marcus shifted his shoulders up and down and smiled. Then he lifted his arms and went "doot-doot-doot" to the rhythm.

"Hey!" I said, putting on a dry T-shirt. "We lost. You forgetting that already?"

"One game," Marcus replied. "Like we've never lost a game before? You've got a short memory if you think that."

Marcus and I have been teammates on and off since first-grade soccer. We played Little League baseball together, YMCA floor hockey, Jaycees basketball, you name it. But this was big-time compared to all of that. Middle school basketball in the best league in the county. I had made the starting lineup right off the bat, displacing an eighth-grade point guard. I'd never felt pressure like this before. But I'd handled it well.

Until tonight.

Coach will probably bench me. I had no business being out there.

I'm more skilled than any guard on the team. But if I can't handle the pressure in a big game like this one, what good am I?

Marcus zipped his gym bag. "You going to sit there all night?"

"I'll be right out," I said. "Tell my dad I'm hungry."

"You? Hungry? He'll be shocked," Marcus said.

Our fathers own an accounting business together, and our families live across the street from each other. So I've known Marcus my whole life.

Marcus left the locker room. Somebody turned off the music, and I hurried to get dressed. Then I heard Coach.

"Good effort tonight, Torry," he said. "You played him tough."

"I felt like a little kid out there," I said.

"We'll get another shot at them in a few weeks," Coach said. "Chalk this one up as a learning experience."

"I guess." I shut my locker. "Thanks, Coach."

"For what?"

"For not giving up on me."

Coach laughed. "Not even close," he said. "Get a good sleep. Tomorrow's a new day."

"Yeah." I like Coach Mancini. He's a young guy, only one year out of college. He works us very hard, but he's fair and gives us the truth. He's always upbeat.

Outside, my breath wafted up in a puff of steam. The January night was freezing cold, but the parking lot was dry. I waved to my father, who was standing next to his car with Marcus's dad. Our fathers are both over six feet tall and still play a lot of basketball, mostly early morning pick-up games at the Y.

I said hi to Mr. Thorpe.

"Tough game," Dad said, shaking his head. "It could have gone either way."

I shrugged and got into the backseat with Marcus. "Could we get something to eat?" I asked. "I didn't have much dinner. Too worked up before the game."

"You guys hungry?" Dad asked.

Marcus and his father said yes.

"Can't do anything that takes too long," Dad said. "You two have school in the morning. Tacos?"

Tacos sounded good. "Yeah."

"Call Mom. Tell her we'll be home soon."

I had to read ten pages in my state history book before bed, and I wanted to start on my science project. But I wouldn't be able to concentrate without some grub first. I sent Mom a text that we'd be a little late.

Mr. Thorpe turned from the front seat. "You really hustled tonight, Torry," he said.

"At least I did that much," I replied.

"Not enough?"

I sighed. "That was embarrassing."

"What was? Losing? Never."

"I got outplayed," I said.

Mr. Thorpe let out a short laugh. "Not so much. That kid has three inches and fifteen pounds on you. And that extra year of experience is huge."

"He's a step quicker, too," Dad added. "You can't learn size. But you can learn defense. We'll work on a few things."

I caught Marcus's eye and gave him a half smile. Marcus rolled his eyes. Our dads are always giving us pointers about basketball. Two-on-two games in the driveway turn into coaching sessions, and games of H-O-R-S-E become shooting demonstrations.

It's supposed to be fun, I thought. And usually it is. Lately I've been getting nervous before games, though. Tonight's loss will probably make that worse.

We reached the outskirts of the downtown where the taco place is. I ordered three chicken tacos. We took a table in the corner.

Marcus said, "That was some noise on that blocked shot. Like the roof was caving in."

I laughed for real. "I'll be hearing that in my sleep. *Thwack!*"

"You did everything right on that play," Dad said. "No worries about that."

I was already starting to feel better about the game. Robertson's an all-star. He led Central to the league title last year. Tonight had been only my sixth game at this level.

"He's good at faking," I said. "I'd overreact and he'd just step back and hit wide-open jumpers."

"So you learned something," Dad said. "Next time, it'll happen less."

I took a big bite of taco. Then I wiped a smear of guac from my chin with the back of my hand. Some of it landed on my sleeve.

"This is called a napkin," Dad joked, tossing one across the table.

I felt my face get warm. I took another bite and made a big show of using the napkin, sweeping it over my mouth. "My legs are fried," I said. "Felt like I was backpedaling the whole game, trying to contain that guy."

"I'm not tired at all," Marcus said. "I wish I were."

The other seventh graders had played in every game except this one. But most of those had been blowouts, so Marcus and the others picked up some late minutes. I was a big reason those games had been out of reach by the fourth quarter.

Coach was right. I'll put this game behind me. I did get schooled, but I'll be better because of that.

I felt a surge of energy and bit into my second taco.

Already I was feeling eager to get back on the court. "Too bad it's so cold out," I said. "Otherwise we could play some two-on-two tonight."

15

TWO

Basketball World

My little sister was still awake when we got home, so I read her a story like I usually do. It's good practice for me, and we both love spending a few minutes together before bedtime.

"So, why didn't you win, Torry?" Nicki asked with a smile. "Were you scared?"

"Nah," I said. "I get nervous before the games, but once the ball is on the court, I don't sweat it. They were just better than us tonight. It'll be different next time."

She chose a book I've read to her many times, about a baby bird searching for its mother. I was glad she didn't choose a book I didn't know.

I had a hard time learning to read, and I still struggle with it. Certain words on the page just don't make sense to me until someone else says them out loud. And I make mistakes sometimes when I try spelling easy words. I know how to spell *orange*, but I wrote *ornage* on a test yesterday in school. I know all the right letters, but sometimes I put them in the wrong order.

My teachers and my parents give me a lot of help, and my reading has improved a ton. But some words just stop me cold.

Nicki let out a yawn as I finished the book. "I'm sleepy," she said. She'd stayed up extra late to see me after the game. That made me feel really good.

My room is next to Nicki's. I have a small basketball hoop hanging above the doorway, and I've smudged up the paint on the wall by bouncing a ball off of it. I picked up a very soft, squishy ball and stepped across the room, eyeing the rim. Then I took a nice easy shot, and it swished.

I swooped in and grabbed the ball, throwing out a few fakes before leaping. I imagined Robertson's long arm reaching to block the shot.

So I
tilted back
just a little more
and banked the ball
into the basket.

Making shots like that is easy
here in my room. It's not so easy
when a real opponent is in your face.

I did it again. And again.

Then I heard a rap on the door.

"It doesn't sound like you're studying
in there," Mom said.

19

I cracked open the door. "It's interactive studying," I said with a grin.

"Oh yeah?" Mom replied. "Which subject would that be?"

"Phys ed?"

"Get a shower and get reading," Mom said. "It's late."

I glanced at the clock. It *was* late. But we only have two evening games on the entire schedule, so this doesn't happen very often.

By the time I finished my reading for history, it was nearly ten o'clock.

My parents were talking in the living room. "All right if I use the computer?" I asked. "It's for school."

"Just a little while," Mom said.

I want to study the planets when I grow up. In fact, I want to visit some of them. Last fall, I did a mural where I painted each of the planets in their order from the sun.

This new project will take me beyond just knowing the planets. Scientists keep discovering places where there might be life on other planets and moons. It turns out Mars has lots of frozen water at its poles. And some of the other planets' moons might have oceans hidden under thick layers of ice. Water is needed for our kind of life. So if there's water out in the solar system, there might also be living things.

My new project will be a map of the solar system, showing the "hot spots" where life might exist. It's my first step toward becoming an astrobiologist. That's a scientist who studies life in outer space.

"Mom!" I called. I'd been staring at the same sentence for what seemed like ten minutes. "What is this word?"

She looked where I pointed. "Uh-mean-oh," she said, pronouncing it. "Amino acids are the building blocks of life."

I blushed. I know what amino acids are. But tonight the word looked sort of like *animal* to me, or *annoying*.

"Thanks," I said. "My brain wasn't working."

Mom kissed the top of my head. "It works fine," she said. "Just a little different. Everyone is different from everybody else."

Very true. I thought about my three best friends—Marcus, Griffin, and Javon. We look about as different as any four guys could look, and we all have our own interests. But we have a lot in common, too. Especially sports.

My parents went up to bed. "Five more minutes, Torry," Dad said as he climbed the stairs. "School tomorrow."

"Right," I said. "Five minutes."

I kept reading. Even if there is water on other worlds, wouldn't it be too cold so far from the sun? But then I read that friction caused by gravity might heat up those moons. And maybe there are creatures that don't need water or oxygen. Before I knew it, it was eleven o'clock. Five minutes had turned into fifty.

I sneaked up the stairs.

I was tired, but when I flopped onto my bed I started thinking about the game. It wasn't that I minded losing. What bothered me was that we could have won. The only real difference was that Robertson had outplayed me.

Badly.

If it were summer, I'd turn on the spotlight and shoot baskets in the driveway. Instead, I scrambled off the bed and picked up the ball.

Quiet, I told myself.

I shifted left, then took a big stride to my right. Up in the air, I slammed the ball down, pulling my hand back just in time to avoid bonking the rim.

The ball fell cleanly through the hoop.

I crossed the room again and faced the rim. I could sense the other players in front of me, hear their breathing, feel the tension. I dribbled low, sliced past Mitchell's screen, and drove to the hoop. Robertson got there a half step too late. I made the shot.

And heard another knock on the door.

I knew who it was. "Hi, Mom."

"More 'studying,' Torry?" she asked.

I opened the door. "More energy."

"Well, three people in this house are trying to sleep. You'd better do the same or we'll be dragging you out of bed in the morning."

"OK," I said, shutting the door as quietly as I could. My parents are used to this. I stay up late a lot of nights, thinking about sports or outer space. Sometimes I listen to soft music until after midnight. That feels almost like sleeping. I crack open the window just slightly and think about my day, sorting out anything that has me bewildered.

Tonight I lay in bed and tried to picture my solar system project, all finished. There was the sun, big and bright. Then tiny Mercury, the closest planet to the sun. Not much chance of life there. Way too hot.

I yawned and closed my eyes. Sleep was definitely on its way.

The next planet out from the sun is Venus. Astronomers think it's even hotter than Mercury. It's almost the same size as Earth, which comes next.

A bigger yawn. Where was I?

Earth. Our home. Floating there in space. Perfectly round. I could squeeze it in my hands. It feels like a basketball. I pivot and leap.

Use the backboard, Torry.

The planet rolls off my fingertips, heading for the hoop. I'm easing into sleep.

Thwack!

I jolt awake. Somebody blocked my shot.

I'll work on that tomorrow. Too tired.

For now I burrow into my pillow and . . . sleep.

THREE

Standing Still

Thunk, thunk, thunk. That's the sound of basketballs bouncing on the gym floor above me. I love that.

Our locker room is right under the gym, and sometimes I stay there for a few seconds and listen before heading up the stairs. Most of the guys were up there already—dribbling and shooting.

For me, the best part of getting ready is standing here alone. Eyes closed. Thinking. Visualizing what I'll do when we scrimmage.

Listening to that *thunk.*

I jumped and let out a very unmanly squeal when someone grabbed my waist.

"Marcus!" I said, bonking him with my forearm. "Jerk."

Marcus laughed and ran up the stairs, with Griffin and Javon right behind him. I shook my head and walked up slowly. *With dignity*, I told myself. *You're a starter.*

But those three were still giggling when I reached the gym, and I started cracking up, too. So much for dignity.

I wiped my mouth and put on a sneer. "I'm supposed to be angry about last night's loss, remember?" I said. "Don't make me laugh. Team leaders mean business."

"Okay, Mr. Serious," Javon said. "Or is it 'All Business Santana'? The man with no sense of humor."

"I'll laugh when we win," I replied. But I couldn't stop smiling. These guys never let me sulk.

Coach had us running right away—line drills and side-to-sides. He said it wasn't punishment for losing. He just wanted us tired before we practiced game-like situations.

"It *feels* like punishment," Marcus whispered to me after the third line drill. Everybody was gasping for breath.

I like sprinting. But I gasped, too.

Coach told Griffin and another guy to take a breather. Neither seemed to be hurting more than the rest of us, but they both get exercise-induced asthma. Their doctors keep it under control, but Coach is extra cautious with them.

We ran three more sprints. Then Coach blew his whistle. "Let's work on the half-court offense." He threw me a bounce pass. The four other starters took their positions, too. Coach put five defenders on the floor, including Marcus.

Eddie Dugan stepped in front of me, down in his stance, arms spread wide. He's an inch shorter than me, not quite as quick, but with some muscles I don't have.

Dugan earned the job as starting point guard midway through last season, and he wasn't happy when I took it away from him this year. He's never said a word to me, but he tests me at every practice. I can't blame him. He believes he should be the starter. A few other eighth graders think that, too. And after last night, I heard a bit of buzzing in the locker room. Like, if Dugan had been covering Robertson, maybe we wouldn't have lost.

I'm not arrogant or anything, but I know I'm better than Dugan. Time to show it. Again.

"Work the ball around," Coach said. "Open man. Open shots."

I took a return pass and started to drive, then stepped back and passed to a man in the corner. The defenders were playing us tight.

The ball came back to me. We're not big, so we tend toward a spread offense, moving the ball around quickly, making lots of cuts. I control the flow, and most passes are either to me or from me.

No one was open. I drove, turned, raised to shoot.

Dugan smacked the ball loose. Marcus grabbed it and dribbled to midcourt.

Coach blew his whistle. "Again."

I passed to the right. Nothing. Took the return pass and threw it left to Wade Barnes.

"Why are we standing still?" Coach yelled.

Our style of offense requires constant motion, constant passing. Coach was right. We weren't moving at all.

"Set some screens!" I called. I took a return pass. "Move!"

Barnes cut to the hoop, but Marcus switched off and picked him up. I drove hard to the right, spun, and looked for Mitchell, who was coming straight down the lane.

I tossed the ball. Marcus batted it down. Dugan grabbed it and dribbled away.

Coach whistled again. "What was that, Torry?"

I looked over.

"Throw bounce passes in that situation. Don't just toss it up for grabs," he said.

Awful start. Two possessions, two turnovers.

"Keep on him, Eddie," an eighth grader mumbled. "You've got him shook up."

Dugan stared me down as I took the ball. I could see the wispy threads of a mustache beginning above his lip.

I dribbled twice, passed to Barnes, and drifted toward the opposite corner. I was open but too far for Barnes to see. He'd already stopped his dribble and was trapped outside. No one came over to help. I hustled back to the top of the key as Marcus tipped a pass and came up with the ball.

"Who's the first team here?" Coach said. "Did you guys forget how to play overnight?"

We stood there flat-footed, staring at the floor.

Coach pointed to Marcus and Dugan. "You five. Switch to offense." He waved toward the bench and looked from me to Barnes and the other starters. "You guys find a seat and pay attention."

Javon, Griffin, and the last three subs came out as defenders.

Coach handed Dugan the ball. "Run the offense," he said. "Our offense. Quick. Sharp. Moving. Unlike that last sequence."

I took a seat on the first row of the bleachers. The four eighth graders sat one row behind me. I could hear them muttering.

Dugan hit a jump shot from the corner.

"Nice, Eddie!" Barnes said.

"Spit him out!" Mitchell added.

I turned and caught Mitchell's eye. He shrugged. I turned back to the court.

Coach let us sit there for a good forty minutes, pretending we didn't count. This bench is where Griffin and Javon and the other deep subs are usually perched during scrimmages, while the first and second teams battle it out. Coach kept heaping praise on the subs, talking about their hustle and their smarts.

He meant all of that for our ears, of course. For not hustling today. For not thinking.

Mitchell slid down one row to sit by me. "Last night stung," he said, looking straight ahead.

"Yeah. But what's wrong with us today?"

"Our brains are dead?" he said. "Coach knows what he's doing. We were chumps out there today. No need to make it worse."

"So this is a day off?" I asked.

"Sort of. I think if we'd been red hot he would have left us out there. But we looked like zombies."

They were scrimmaging full-court now. Dugan drained a long three-pointer and stuck his fist in the air.

"You the man, Eddie!" Mitchell yelled. Then he turned to me and lowered his voice. "So Coach goes with the guys with the energy today."

"How do you know all this?"

"My dad tells me stuff. He knows how coaches think. He played a lot of ball."

I nodded. "Mine, too."

Mitchell said, "Coach'll let us think we're in the doghouse. But really, he's giving us a break."

I jutted my head back toward the eighth graders behind me. "They know?" I whispered.

Mitchell smiled and shook his head. "They think our starting jobs are in jeopardy. So they'll go twice as hard the next time they hit the court."

"You think that's Coach's strategy?" I asked.

Mitchell tapped his forehead. "The brain. Big part of basketball."

Marcus scored on a nice give-and-go from Dugan. Marcus was playing out of his mind today, racking up steals, assists, and lay-ups. Not much difference between our first five and the next five.

"All right," Coach said. "Excellent scrimmage. That's enough for today, since we ran first. Everybody take ten free throws and we're done."

I headed for one of the side baskets. The eighth graders always shoot first, so I'd be rebounding for a few minutes.

"Starters, stay behind," Coach said.

I winced. Coach never gets mad, but he'd never benched all of us either. I hoped Mitchell's theory was right.

"You were way off today," he said as the five of us sat against the wall. "Flat. Careless. Disinterested!"

We all shifted a little. I tried to keep my eyes on Coach.

"One loss doesn't hurt us," he said. "But I guarantee those guys from Central weren't dragging their tails in practice today. They're looking forward. Like you need to do."

Mitchell slowly raised his hand. "Are we still the starters?"

"Of course," Coach said. "But let's see a big difference tomorrow. And especially in Thursday's game."

When we reached the locker room, the music was blaring. Dugan stood near his locker, joking with some of the other eighth graders.

"Hot hand," Mitchell said, punching Dugan's shoulder.

Dugan nodded. He saw me looking at him and scowled. He turned away and whacked Mitchell in return.

I get it. Dugan had a great day in practice. So what? We all have those. It's the games that count. I'm still the starter. Coach just said so.

Marcus inched over to me and acted all serious. "Think you'll ever play again?" he asked.

I knew he was busting on me. "No," I said. I gave him my most depressed look. "We're off the team."

His eyes went wide. "Get out!" he said.

I stared at the floor and shook my head slowly, acting all heartbroken. Then I looked up and laughed. "You bought that? Man, are you gullible."

"Great acting," Marcus said. "Honestly, that would have been awesome news for me. I'd be a starter."

He was kidding, of course. But that's just the way we talk to each other. We say serious things, but if you're listening to us, don't ever take the words at face value. We usually say the opposite of what we mean.

"I feel so bad for you," I said. See?

"Watch out," Marcus replied. "We played well today."

"Against the third string."

"Still."

Griffin and Javon were ready to leave. We all live in the same neighborhood, so we walk back and forth together most of the time. "Let's get out of here," I said to Marcus.

Then I put a hand up to stop him. "You did play great today," I said.

I meant what I said that time.

FOUR

Glued to the Bench

It's a funny thing. I'd done less in practice than usual, but I was hungrier than ever. "Let's hit the bagel place," I said as we left the locker room.

"It's two blocks out of the way," Javon complained. He pulled his cap down over his ears, which stick out a bit. Javon is the smallest of us.

"So what? I need fuel," I said. I started walking up the dark side street toward Main.

"How's the homework load?" Griffin asked. "Anybody up for some games tonight at my house?" Griffin's smart at tech stuff. He likes beating us soundly at video games.

I had very little homework, but I couldn't wait to get back into my planet project. There were some great websites I'd barely looked at yet.

"I've got a lot of science to work on," I said.

"Really?" Marcus asked. "We're all in the same class, bro. We don't have any."

"The project, man."

"Oh. Right. We have ten days. What's the hurry?"

"Because I love it."

The cold wind hit us hard as we turned onto Main. Bagelworks is between Second and Third Streets, next to a pizza place and a Mexican restaurant. Our dads' accounting office is across the street on the second floor, above a florist. Looked like they were still open.

We entered the bagel shop, and I ordered a cinnamon-raisin to go. The bins were nearly empty, so no one had much to choose from. The place would be closing soon, at six o'clock.

I talked about my project as we walked home. "I'll draw what I think the life-forms might look like on each planet or moon," I said. I'd sketched some funny drawings in a notebook during school today—bacteria with goofy faces and little blue hats.

"Are you going to have flying saucers, Torry?" Javon asked. "And little green Martians with big eyes and antennae?"

"It's not like that," I said.

"I got over Martians in, like, second grade," Javon said. "Right after dinosaurs."

Griffin laughed. "Alien abductions! You can show a big fleet of spaceships flying toward Earth."

"I don't think so," I said. I told them that other life in our solar system would probably be tiny. Like yeast or molds. In the bigger oceans there might be simple animals like jellyfish.

"I think creatures on Venus are smarter than we are," Javon said.

"First of all, I don't think there are any creatures on Venus," I said. "But I agree that any bacteria out in space are probably smarter than you."

"Ha ha," Javon replied. "Seriously, Torry, this project sounds babyish. Martians and spaceships?"

"I just said it isn't about that. This is real science." But I did hope to make cool drawings.

"I drew pictures like that in kindergarten," Javon said. "Flying dogs from outer space!" He was cracking himself up. Griffin was laughing, too.

"Forget it," I said. "You'll see it when it's finished." I changed the subject to basketball. Said they'd all played pretty well today.

"How'd you like the view from my world?" Javon asked. "Glued to the bench all practice."

I shrugged. "It's interesting. You see things from the sidelines that you miss on the court."

"Like what? What a great shooter I am?" Javon rose from his feet and mimed a jump shot. He'd made one shot all day, as I recalled. Took about seven others that missed.

"You see plays developing," I said. "Actually, you see how plays should develop but don't. How a little more awareness would lead to much better passing and driving."

"That's what Coach is always saying," Marcus said.

Javon took another air shot. "I don't like thinking on the court," he said. "Just let it flow naturally. That's my game."

And that's why you're a third stringer, I thought.

"Dugan was saying some things," Griffin said. Javon gave him a nudge.

"What things?" I asked, though I could guess.

"Just things," Griffin said. "You gotta admit, he played great today."

"He's a good player," I said, being all generous and humble. I could be mad about not playing today, but I wasn't. Not much.

"I made Dugan look good," Marcus said. "Every time he scored, he had me to thank for an assist."

We crossed Prospect Avenue, and Javon and Griffin headed for their street. Then they stopped.

"Hey, Torry," Javon said.

I looked at him and waited.

He stared back. "Don't turn into an old man or something, you know?"

"What?"

"This big science thing, and your 'team leader' idea." Javon swung his gym bag. "You're still just one of us. You hear me?"

That caught me by surprise. "I hear." But I didn't quite get it. Or maybe I did.

"Later," Javon said.

"Tomorrow."

Marcus and I walked another block in silence. As we neared our houses, I said, "So what did Dugan say?"

"The usual stuff. You know, 'Coach'll finally wise up and start me.' That sort of thing."

"Think it could happen?"

Marcus stopped in front of his house. "It shouldn't. But that's up to you. No coach would stick with a guy who isn't performing. But you are . . . were. . . y'know. Just get back to it next game."

I nodded. "Thursday's game. Clean slate."

"All right." Marcus started up the walk.

"Do you think my alien-life thing sounds stupid?" I asked.

"I didn't say that. They did."

"What do you think?"

"It's cool. Whatever."

"Right. See you in the morning."

Now I had two things I could be mad about: Dugan thinking he can take my job away and those guys making fun of my project.

But I brightened up as soon as I saw Nicki. She was looking out a front window, waiting for me to get home. I always used to wait for Dad like that. Now she waits for him and me. Mom gets out of work earlier and picks Nicki up from day care.

"Hey, Nicki. Did you make dinner?"

"Mommy did."

"Did you help?"

She shook her head.

"You can help me set the table. Come on."

At dinner, Dad kept asking me about practice. I think a big part of him wishes he was still in school, playing on a team. I like talking to him about basketball. Usually. Not so much today.

"So?" he said after I mumbled something about having an off day. "What's that mean? Your shots hit the side of the backboard?"

I chewed a hunk of chicken, then took a sip of milk. "Coach mostly sat the starters today. To give us a break, I think."

"Did he say he was giving you a break?"

"Not really . . . Mitchell did."

Mom piped in. "What made him think that?"

I set down my fork and tapped my fingers on the table. I shrugged. "He just thought so."

Dad scrunched up his mouth, then let out his breath. "If a coach benches his starters, it's a pretty good sign he isn't happy. I wouldn't count it as a break."

"He didn't think we were hustling today."

"Was he right?"

"I hustled," I said. "I always hustle. But yeah, there wasn't much action."

Dad reached for another spoonful of rice. "Chalk it up," he said. "You learned something."

His favorite expression. I nodded. Then I grinned. "So, what did you learn today, Dad?"

"Say what?"

"What did you learn? You always say I need to learn something new every day. Does that end when you finish school or what?"

Dad laughed. "I learned that my son can be a wise guy. But, okay, let's see. I learned . . . I don't know. Maybe nothing."

"How about you, Mom? Learn anything today?"

Mom wiped her mouth with a napkin. "I certainly did. I learned a new shortcut on the computer at work. It'll save me fifteen seconds every time I scan a document."

"See?" I said. "Mom learned something. I learned something. I bet Nicki learned a hundred things at preschool."

"We learned a new song," Nicki said.

"Poor Dad," I joked, shaking my head. "You're being left behind in the learning department."

"Guess I'd better get on the computer," he said. "I've still got a few hours before the day is over."

"I'll join you," I said. "Let's look up Europa. One of Jupiter's moons. They learn new things about it all the time."

"I accept," Dad said. "Time for me to get schooled, too."

FIVE

Every Second

The bus ride to Thursday's game at Kennedy took only fifteen minutes, but it felt like the longest of my life. Marcus kept trying to get me to talk, but when I'm tense, I just zone everything out.

"You in there?" he said, waving a hand in front of my face.

I frowned, looking out the window. We'd barely beat Kennedy in the first game of the season. The guy I'd be guarding today was a great shooter and fast. He'd burned me a few times in the opener.

I seemed to be the only one on the bus who was nervous. The eighth graders were bunched up toward the back, laughing and yelling.

In the warm-up drill, I missed my first lay-up. I trotted back into line and fist-bumped Marcus.

Barnes threw me a pass. I juked left, then spun to the free-throw line and swished a jumper. I made my next two shots. Started sweating. Felt a surge of energy and confidence.

Like always, put a ball in my hands and the jitters just flow away.

So I didn't worry when I dribbled the ball off my foot on our first possession. And I kept my cool as Derek Lang dropped in a couple of three-pointers and Kennedy jumped to a quick 11–4 lead.

Coach called time-out. I saw Dugan by the scorer's table as I jogged toward the bench.

"Quick rest, Torry," Coach said.

I squeezed between Griffin and Javon on the bench.

"You'll be right back out there," Griffin said.

I pulled up the front of my jersey and wiped my face. "Better be."

Javon nudged me with his elbow. "You've gotta settle down, Torry," he said. "Lang's not that good.

You should be eating him up, but they're totally killing us."

Dugan played the rest of the quarter, and he helped trim the lead to four points. We gathered around Coach. "Keep cutting," Coach said. "Keep up the defensive pressure." He pointed to Marcus. "Report in for Barnes."

Wait a minute. Marcus was going in before me?

It worked. Marcus and Dugan had played well together in practice all week, and it continued here. They each got a steal, sparking fast-break lay-ups that evened the score.

It went back and forth from there, both teams clicking on offense.

Coach finally told Barnes and me to report back in with three minutes left in the half. I kneeled at the scorer's table and waited for a stoppage. It was good to see Marcus getting the playing time. He'd earned it. But where did I stand now? I'd spent most of the half on the bench.

Time to step it up, I told myself.

Finally the ref called a foul and Lang went to the free-throw line.

The buzzer sounded for the substitution. I pointed to Dugan, and he ran to the bench with Marcus. The rest of the team stood up and clapped. Dugan had played better than I had.

Right back into it, Torry, like you never sat down.

All my senses get sharper as soon as the ball's in play. I felt each dribble intensely in my fingers, heard each squeak of my sneakers, and locked in on Lang's eyes as he tried to stare me down.

I hit Mitchell in the paint, and he pivoted and banked in a lay-up. Then Barnes and I zeroed in on Lang, trapping him in the backcourt and forcing him to throw away the ball.

Another bucket. We had the lead. But Lang hit a jumper in the final seconds to pull within a point at the half.

Kennedy doesn't have a locker room for visiting teams, so Coach took us out into the hallway and we leaned against some lockers.

"Great guard play," he said. "We'll keep that rotation, with Eddie and Marcus getting minutes."

I didn't blink. But what I heard was Coach reducing my playing time. The more Dugan played,

the less I would. I'd been in for 99 percent of the key minutes this season. Today I hadn't played half.

But we were winning. That's what mattered. Right?

Back in the gym, I tried to keep my intensity up. The great thing about being the starting point guard all season was that as long as I performed,

nobody would take away my job. Now that possibility was right there.

"Starting five," Coach said as we huddled up. At least I'd get another chance.

Bring it on.

Poor Lang. He never knew what hit him. I played ten times harder. I stole two passes, ignited a couple of fast breaks, and drained a three-pointer from the corner. By the time the Kennedy coach called time-out, we were ahead by eight.

We didn't let up. Biggest quarter of the season. With just over a minute left, Dugan came in for me. He did something surprising, too. He gave me a fist bump as he took the court.

I sat next to Marcus.

"I think you made your point," he said.

I nodded. "I was fired up. Not ready to lose my job, that's for sure."

"Nobody on this team can play like you do," Marcus said. "Coach knows that."

I'd still played less than half a game, but we were running away with it. I'd shown my value. So I sat and enjoyed watching the play. I even tried to appreciate what Dugan contributed.

When Lang fouled out, Kennedy's last hopes seemed to end. Coach waved his hand toward Javon and Griffin and they ran onto the court.

"Javon!" I called. He was still wearing his warm-up jersey. He blushed, pulled it over his head, and tossed it to me. Then he scored a couple of baskets as we locked up the win.

"That was a total team effort," Coach said on the bus. "Great balance. Great play off the bench. Big contributions from the nonstarters."

Marcus gave me a thumbs-up. "He means me," he said. "Looks like I'll be playing more."

It also meant Dugan. Which meant I'd be playing less. But Coach had been relying on five guys for most of the season. Good teams have a lot more depth than that. So this was progress.

"Look at it this way," Marcus said. "If you get a little more rest during the games, you'll have that much more energy when you're on the court. Every second will be intense."

"Probably," I said. It's true that I can get winded playing an entire game. Today I'd had no letdowns, took advantage of every minute of play.

"As long as we're winning," I said. But I wasn't quite convinced. I wanted to play every second.

The bus turned onto Main Street, and I noticed that my dad's office light was still on. So when we got to school I just threw my stuff into my backpack and headed up there.

"Big win?" Dad said when I poked my head in.

"Yeah. Good one."

"I'm almost done here," he said, tapping a few keys on his computer. He was the last one left in the office. "Better defense today?"

"Offense, defense. Everything clicked. It was close at the half, but then we clobbered them."

"And it was *fun*?" We both forget that part of it sometimes, as Mom keeps reminding us.

"It was." At least it was fun when I played. Watching is less fun. Especially when somebody's trying to take your job away.

"Sorry I missed it," Dad said. "I'll be there next time."

I told him that Marcus had contributed a lot today. "Coach wants to get more participation from the bench."

"Good idea, in theory. As long as you have the horses for it."

"I think we do. I played less than usual, but there wasn't any drop-off once we got rolling." Part of me wished there had been. I wanted there to be a clear contrast between me and Dugan.

I'd just have to outplay him again in practice.

SIX

Driveway Lessons

On Saturday afternoon, I made a list of all the places in the solar system that might have life. Thinking about what that life would look like was the coolest part of the project. I drew funny cartoon sketches, but there's serious science behind all this.

Tiny life-forms are the most likely beings in the cold outer reaches of space. But drawings of bacteria are boring, even if I put funny faces on them. The idea of the project is to show where there might be life and why, not what it looks like. So I could have fun inventing creatures for each place, even if they were farfetched.

I started with gas giant Jupiter's moons. It has more than sixty! The moon Io has red spots like tomato sauce and dark spots that look like olives.

I got out my drawing pencils.

"Are you drawing dinner?" Nicki asked, peeking around me to look at the sketch.

"Looks tasty, huh? But it's a moon, not a pizza."

I made a second drawing of Io, with a big chunk cut away to show the inside. Those dark spots on the surface are from huge volcanoes that erupt constantly, so anything living there would have to be really tough to survive.

I figured that the tubes the volcanic lava erupted through would stay hot. Maybe some life-form had developed in those tubes. It could find a way to cling to the solid rock and not be disturbed by the eruptions.

I drew little creatures with sticky feet. They looked like frogs with big toe pads and long fingers for holding on to the rocky walls. And I gave them umbrellas to make the lava bounce away. It was funny, but it was like real science.

"They're cute!" Nicki said.

"They wouldn't really have umbrellas," I said. "But they would need a natural shield. Like turtles and lobsters have, with their hard shells."

Another of Jupiter's moons probably has liquid water. The coolest thing about Ganymede is that it's like a giant sandwich, with a layer of ice at the surface, then a layer of water below that, then

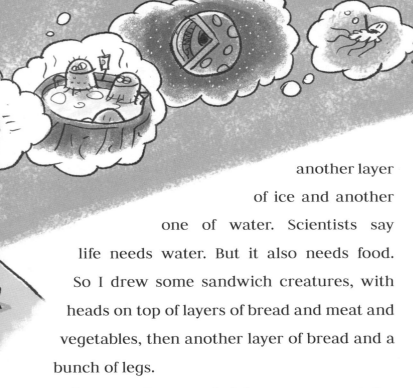

another layer
of ice and another
one of water. Scientists say
life needs water. But it also needs food.
So I drew some sandwich creatures, with
heads on top of layers of bread and meat and
vegetables, then another layer of bread and a
bunch of legs.

"The medium sandwich creatures eat the
littlest ones," I said. "The biggest sandwiches eat
the medium ones.

"Do they really look like that?" Nicki asked.

"Nah. But a sandwich world might have
sandwich people, right?"

Nicki said the sandwich people made her
hungry. She headed to the kitchen for a snack.

"Would you bring me a banana?" I asked.

Jupiter has two more moons that might have life. Europa and Callisto probably have oceans under a surface of ice. The ice shields the water so it doesn't freeze all the way down to the ground. And volcanoes from the core heat up that water, too. On Earth, there are creatures that live so deep in the ocean that sunlight never reaches them. They thrive near volcanic vents. So the same thing could happen on those moons.

I drew some jellyfish in Europa's ocean. With big smiles and glasses of iced tea, they were relaxing in a hot tub next to a volcanic vent.

Too babyish? I didn't think so. Javon and Griffin would probably make fun of it, but I felt creative.

Nicki handed me an orange. "We're out of bananas."

Peeling the orange would make my fingers sticky, and I didn't want any of that on my drawings. I held up the orange and turned it around. The thick outer skin was like a crust of ice on a moon. Under that crust was a protected layer—probably water—where things could swim and breathe.

"Aren't you going to eat it?" Nicki asked.

"Soon," I said. "But that orange reminded me of something." I handed it to Nicki. "What does it look like?"

"The sun?"

"Yeah. But something really important to me. Round, orange . . ."

Nicki smiled. "A basketball!"

The weather had turned a little warmer, and I was antsy from sitting at my desk. I put on a sweatshirt and went outside.

The driveway was damp from melted snow, but it didn't slow me down. I shot a dozen free throws, then worked on lay-ups and short jumpers. It always feels good to have a ball in my hands.

The sounds got my dad's attention. I just wanted to shoot, but I figured I'd listen to him.

"That rematch with Central is next Friday, right?" he asked.

I nodded. I'd have to cover Robertson again. I was ready, but there was no need to lay awake at night worrying about it.

Dad rebounded a shot and walked up the driveway to a spot about twenty feet from the hoop. "Get in your stance," he said.

I faced him and got in my defensive stance, thinking about the basics. Usually it comes naturally, but I figured he would test me, so I thought through the main points. Balanced on my feet, crouched low with my shoulders above my knees, hands up.

Dad dribbled a couple of times, then darted right, pulled back, and gave a head fake. I reached for the ball. He lunged left, then took a half step back and shot. I fell for the lunge, so he had an easy shot.

"Again," Dad said.

This time he got me with a lunge to the right, and he made another easy jumper.

When we lined up for another go, Dad patted the front of his sweatshirt. "Look here, Torry."

The shirt said KNICKS. I read it out loud.

"Here," he said. "My waist. I faked you out because you were watching everything but that. A player can move his hands, his feet, the ball, but he's not going anywhere without his waist."

That made sense.

"That's why Robertson was able to lose you so easily," Dad said. "The guy makes one move after another. You're not going to stop him every time. But you'll get beat a lot less if you watch his waist."

Dad burned me a few more times, but I managed to contain him, too. The tip definitely worked. I stopped overreacting to his moves. He's inches taller than I am and just as quick, so I couldn't shut him down. But I wasn't being thrown off balance every time he lunged and stepped back.

"Enough," Dad said.

"But I'm just getting warmed up."

"Life is more than basketball," he replied. Then he broke into a big smile. He knows as well as I do that we put too much emphasis on hoops sometimes. Even most of our shirts and caps say CELTICS or SPURS or UCLA.

I felt a little more confident about guarding Robertson again. But I knew that would be different from trying to stop my dad in the driveway. He plays hard against me, but he's still my father. He'd never demolish me the way another kid would. Dad would let up a little if he saw that I was getting down.

Robertson wouldn't. He'd keep scoring and passing and stealing the ball. The only way I'd get relief from that would be for Coach to bench me.

"Ten more minutes?" I said to Dad.

He laughed. "You wore me out. Let's eat lunch. We'll play more basketball tomorrow."

SEVEN

Hogging It

I kept looking at the clock on Monday, waiting for the school day to end. Couldn't wait to get on the court. First chance to go head-to-head against Dugan for a while. I had a lot to prove.

Finally. I gathered my books and headed for the locker room. Marcus fell into step beside me. "Did you hibernate all weekend?" he asked.

"I was doing artwork for my science project. And shooting free throws."

"You are intense," Marcus said. "This project isn't supposed to be so major."

"I'm into it."

Javon and Griffin came around the corner, heading to the same place we were. "Into what?" Javon asked. "Cartoon Martians again?"

"Something like that," I said. I wasn't about to give them another chance to mock the project. It was almost done, and I'd be presenting it to the class on Friday. "You guys ready for some hard hoops today?"

"Shouldn't be too hard," Griffin said. "Coach doesn't run us ragged the day before a game."

I was so focused on covering Robertson on Friday I'd forgotten that we had a game the next day. Not a good idea. You should never look past any opponent unless you want a rude awakening.

Coach did run us hard. We were scrimmaging full-court ten minutes into practice. And Dugan was giving me trouble. Dad's tip about watching the waist was working well, but Dugan must have learned some things over the weekend, too. I wasn't able to drive past him into the lane as easily as before.

He was back to his old attitude—no eye contact, not responding if I said anything to him.

Still, I was playing well. The main role of the point guard is to run the offense—to get the ball into the hands of anybody who can score. I did that and even picked up a basket here and there.

So I was surprised when Coach stopped the scrimmage and had Dugan and me switch sides.

"Eddie, get some time with the starters," he said. He didn't give any explanation, but it was clear I should step over to the second team.

Marcus gave me a fist bump. He was excited that we'd be playing in the same unit. I wasn't.

I didn't expect a big change. I was still guarding Dugan, and he was still guarding me. He had better players to work with now, but I'd had that advantage, too.

If the second team starts outplaying the first, I'll be the reason, I thought. *Coach will notice that, for sure.*

So as soon as I got the ball, I revved up my game. I made a quick juke, got past Dugan, and drove to the hoop. Nobody set a screen, though, and I stopped short when Mitchell blocked my path.

I had no shot. No one was open. Marcus ran to me, and I bounced the ball toward him. Dugan grabbed it first and raced up the court, hitting Barnes for an easy lay-up.

It happened again. I drove, got stopped, and made a less-than-perfect pass.

Steal. Fast break. Lay-up.

We got trounced. The starting four plus Dugan rolled up the score and shut us down nearly every time we had the ball.

I belong over there, I kept telling myself. I'd never played with the second team before. I should have been the one with those steals.

At the end of practice, Coach had me take a seat on the bleachers.

I stared straight out at the court, leaning against the row behind me.

"You never passed the ball today until you had to," Coach said. "There were four other guys on your side."

I shrugged. "Yeah, but . . ."

"But they're not as good as your usual team?"

I sat up straighter. "Not quite?"

"Let me ask you something," Coach said. "Most days, when we scrimmage, the first and second teams are fairly evenly matched, right? The starters take control, but the competition is close."

"Right."

"So what was the difference today? The starters dominated every aspect of the game."

I thought it over. The only difference was me.

"Eddie runs the second team every day," Coach said. "Does a good job."

"You think he's better than I am?"

"I didn't say that. But he's better at making the best of the team he has to work with. You tried to be a one-man show today. That didn't work."

I let out a long breath.

"Go shoot your free throws with everyone else," Coach said. He stepped onto the court, then turned to face me. "Just think about what went on today. Absorb it and learn from it."

Learn something new every day.

"Coach?"

He knew what I wanted to ask. "The lineup stays the same," he said. "You're the starter."

You wouldn't have known it from the locker room. The eighth graders were gathered around Eddie's locker, laughing and acting like the rightful starter was back. They all figured today had clinched it. But the starting job belonged to me. At least for now.

Coach hadn't said, "You're probably still the starter" or "We'll give you one more chance." He said I was the starter. Period.

I got dressed fast and headed out. Marcus, Javon, and Griffin were waiting on the steps.

We didn't say a word for two blocks. That's not like us at all.

Marcus cleared his throat. "What'd he say?" he asked.

"Who?" I knew he meant Coach Mancini.

We walked another block before I broke the silence.

"He said I'm the starter."

"Really?" Javon asked. "Because everyone was acting like . . ."

"Like they don't know what they're talking about," I said. "He said I'm starting tomorrow. No equivocation."

"No what?" they all said.

"Look it up," I replied. "No doubt. No hesitation. No double meaning. Just a straightforward statement. I'm the starter."

"Equivocation," Marcus repeated. "Sounds like a word your father would use." He was right.

"No waffling, huh?" Marcus added.

"Not a hint of it."

"I like waffles," Javon added. "Mmm, boy, do I like waffles."

I whacked him with my sleeve. We'd reached Prospect, so Javon and Griffin turned off.

"Seriously," Marcus said, "it looked like Coach was making a big change today. Doesn't seem justified, but everybody was convinced Dugan had won his job back."

"Let 'em think what they want. Coach said I played terrible today, regardless of which team I was on. But he definitely did not demote me. In fact, I think he thinks I'll be better because of it. That I learned something about being selfish."

"Did you?" Griffin asked.

"Maybe. I mean, a point guard has to be selfish sometimes. Or at least not entirely democratic, if you know what I mean. You don't have four teammates out there with equal skills. You have to know who can do what."

"Dude, I can do a lot," Marcus said. "But I can't do much if you never pass the ball. None of us can."

"I was hogging it?"

"Oink, oink," Marcus said, making a pig face.

Marcus and I turned off for our street.

"Wait," Marcus said. "Coach never once tried to correct what you were doing today. He just let you keep making the same mistakes over and over."

That was true.

"He must have thought you were smart enough to figure it out on your own, man," Marcus said.

OINK!!

OINK !!

OINK!

That was probably true, too. I laughed. It wasn't all that funny. I was laughing at myself.

Marcus laughed, too. "But you didn't."

"Didn't what?"

"Figure it out."

I kicked at a stone in the street. It popped off the curb. "I would have. Later. I'm not that clueless."

"Right. Tomorrow, make it a blowout. Javon and Griffin want playing time, too."

I knew what I wanted. Dinner. Shower. Thinking time. Time to sort out what I'd learned today.

Time to figure it out and make sure it sticks.

EIGHT

Too Many Guards

The night was calm. I looked out my window at bedtime and noticed that a very light snow was falling—just a few flakes drifting down.

My parents had turned in already, so the house was quiet. I lay flat in my bed under a heap of covers. Warm. Thinking.

I worked on the big poster for my science project tonight, showing the planets and their moons and the asteroids. All of the key places for life are labeled.

Mom asked me why I'd drawn a piece of fruit on the outer edge of the solar system. She pointed to the label: PLUOT.

It took me a few seconds to get her joke, which had happened because of that letter-switching thing I do. A pluot is a cross between a plum and an apricot. Pluto is the farthest planet from the sun, although it no longer has the full status of a planet. Astronomers insist it's just a dwarf planet.

Fortunately, fixing the label was easy.

Pluto is tiny, but it has at least five moons. It's so far from the sun that it seems impossible that it could have any life. But scientists have these really clear pictures of it now. And some of them think it might have a hidden underground ocean. They're learning new stuff all the time. I gave Pluto some icy-blue snow creatures, just for fun.

I turned my thoughts to tomorrow's game. How long was my leash? I trusted Coach that I'd be starting, but what if I messed up early? Would he yank me after two minutes or let me settle in again?

I told myself just to play my game. But would I keep looking at the scorer's table, making sure Dugan wasn't reporting in to replace me? Getting distracted by that would be the worst thing I could do. I had to maintain my focus. But could I?

I glanced at the clock. I should have been asleep, but I was wide awake. Very. I was so awake that I could have played the entire basketball game right then. A big part of me wished I could.

I swung my legs out of bed and looked out the window again. The lawn had a thin layer of snow, but the street was just wet.

What was I worried about? Dugan was pushing me hard. If I didn't keep my game way up, he'd be starting in no time. But basketball's a team sport. My part in it was just that, a part. I should be happy to be a sub if it meant the team would do better.

But that wasn't how I felt. I liked being the only seventh-grade starter. I liked everybody at school knowing I'd earned that. And I loved looking up at the packed bleachers at our games. When I had the ball, all eyes were on me. That felt great. I never wanted to let it go.

I watched the street for a long time. I told myself I'd stay by the window until a car came by, but our street is quiet and none ever came.

Eventually I crawled back into bed.

Finally ready for sleep.

"Torry!" Marcus called, clapping as he waited for my pass. I put some spin on the ball and it bounced into his hands. I trotted into the lay-up line.

Everybody was loose today, slapping hands and moving quickly during warm-ups. The bleachers were filling quickly.

Down the other end of the court, the Eastside team was running a passing drill. Their maroon and silver uniforms looked electric. The entire gym seemed high-energy today. Or was it me?

Coach hadn't announced the starters yet, but I think every eighth grader was expecting Dugan to get the call. He was acting all confident and smart, winking at his friends in the bleachers.

Coach waved us over. I was so jittery I could puke.

"Man-to-man, as always," he said. "Pressure defense. Smart passes and lots of movement." He turned his head and looked at the Eastside players for a second. He tugged at his orange tie with the thin blue stripes. School colors.

"The usual starting five, except Marcus we need you for just the first minute. Joey's getting his knee rewrapped," he said.

Dugan's expression didn't change. He always has the hint of a frown.

I swallowed hard. Blinked a few times.

"Hands in," Coach said.

"1, 2, 3 . . . Let's go!"

I swung my arms. Hopped up and down a few times. Made sure my laces were snug.

I glanced up at the bleachers.

My parents and Nicki were squeezing into the top row next to Marcus's mom and dad.

Focus, I told myself.

Mitchell won the opening jump, tapping the ball safely back to me. As soon as my fingers gripped that ball, I felt the electricity.

I dribbled to the top of the key. Passed the ball to Barnes. Took the return pass.

And shot.

The ball bounced off the rim and Eastside's center grabbed the easy rebound. I sprinted back and found their point guard, settling in on defense.

I shouldn't have taken that shot. I wasn't wide open, and we hadn't tried to penetrate at all.

So after Eastside scored I found some patience. Lots of passes and cutting to the lane. I set a screen.

We scored.

The pace was quick, with both teams moving the ball around and racing up and down the court. We were tied at ten apiece before I knew it. There hadn't been a single whistle until Mitchell got hacked going in for a lay-up.

The buzzer went off. I frowned when I saw Dugan reporting in.

Javon stood up and Griffin held out his palm as I reached the bench. I shoved between them and took a seat, not sure what I should be feeling.

"Nice work," Griffin said. "You took charge."

"So why am I out?" I wiped my face with a towel. Someone handed me a paper cup of water.

"You'll be back," Javon said. "The pace is insane. Even I'm tired, and all I did was sit here."

I was surprised to see that I'd been in the game for more than six minutes. The first quarter was nearly over. Coach had sent in two more subs, so it wasn't just me.

We huddled up at the break, and Coach went back to the starting lineup. Except for me, that is.

"What's going on?" I mumbled as we sat back down. "I played good."

"Him, too," Marcus said, referring to Dugan. We'd built a three-point lead.

Why does Marcus always have to be so reasonable? I gave him a gentle kick in the ankle.

I sat there steaming for what seemed like forever. But halfway through the quarter, Coach told me to report in.

And he sent Marcus with me.

"This'll be like my driveway," I said as we kneeled by the table. "Two-on-two against our dads."

Marcus smiled. He and I almost never played at the same time for this team.

"Lots of passing," I said. "Set screens."

Marcus nodded.

I gave Barnes a high-five as he passed me on the way to the bench. Dugan didn't look my way.

Our lead was four.

Marcus got a steal in the first couple of seconds, and I took off for the basket. He heaved a nice pass that I grabbed on the first bounce. Two dribbles to the hoop and an easy lay-up.

"Pressure!" Coach called. We hadn't put on a full-court press all game, but I turned and shielded the inbounds passer. Marcus shadowed the point guard, so the pass went toward the corner. We had the guard trapped, and he frantically looked for an outlet. He tried to throw a long pass, but I smacked it down. Marcus scooped up the ball as I cut to the hoop.

Quick pass. Another lay-up. Eight-point lead.

Same pressure. They couldn't get the ball in and called for a time-out.

I clapped my hands once and ran to the bench.

"Nice," Coach said. "Back off this time and pick up at half-court. But next time we score, go into the press again. Let's build that lead."

The only big difference between this and playing two-on-two with our dads was that we were dominating. By half time I'd scored three more baskets and the lead was thirteen points.

Coach singled out Marcus at half time. "You keep earning more time, Thorpe," he said. "We've got four strong guards now. That's a nice luxury."

Nice for the team. Nice for me? I could see my minutes slipping away even further if Coach went with a four-guard rotation.

But I liked seeing Marcus get some props. So I adjusted my attitude as Coach shifted us four guards in and out during the second half. I worked well with Barnes and Marcus. Dugan did, too.

The one combination he never tried was Dugan and me at the same time. Two point guards is one too many.

The final score was a landslide, and I had a season-high seventeen points. Not bad for only two-thirds of a game.

I was used to playing more. And I had a big target coming up on the calendar. Friday against Central. Miles Robertson.

Big rematch. A chance for redemption from my only bad game all season.

I didn't want to share that job with anyone.

"No appetite, Torry?" Mom asked at dinner Thursday night. I'd been staring at my plate of pasta for ten minutes.

I stuck a fork in a ravioli but didn't lift it to my mouth. "I'm thinking," I said.

"I wonder what about," Mom said with a smile. "The game will get here soon enough. Eat."

I let out my breath and took a bite. I could still hear that blocked shot from the last time I played against Robertson. Still see him draining those three-pointers over my outstretched fingertips.

"You've come a long way," Dad said. "It's okay to think about the game, but don't let it make you freeze up. You'll be fine as soon as you hit the court."

That was true. But the game was twenty hours away. I had a different worry first: presenting the science project tomorrow morning.

I took another forkful of ravioli. Tasted good. Ate it all. I even had a second helping.

After dinner, I looked over my project. It just needed a few finishing touches—colors here and there and written explanations about some of the life-forms. They looked great, especially the school of underwater pigs I added to one of Jupiter's moons. Why pigs? There were ten of them, and they were all chasing one basketball. They were ball hogs, get it? Like I was sometimes.

Perfect.

I went to my room early and listened to music, lying on my bed and staring at the ceiling. The funny thing is, I like being nervous before a presentation or a game. I enjoy turning inward, just going away by myself and focusing. I do it in the locker room, or on the bus, or even on the court while we're warming up. Just staying quiet and zoning in on the job.

But when I think about how I'll perform, I get an energy surge. That's great when it happens in the minutes before a game. It's a lot less helpful just before bedtime.

I needed to move, to shake off some of that energy. I had two huge hurdles to clear tomorrow. No way could I sleep.

So I went downstairs.

"Okay if I go out and shoot baskets?" I asked.

"It's late," Mom said.

"I know."

"Don't be loud. Your sister's asleep."

I didn't plan on being loud. This was part of the focus. That alone time. It helps to be moving, even if it's just some easy free throws.

The moon shone bright, and the night was strangely warm. I didn't even need a sweatshirt.

I dribbled a couple of times. Shot the ball.

No running. Just the motions.

Thunk. Thunk. Thunk.

I felt warm. For a while I sat on the back step and held the basketball, looking at the rim and the backboard and the moon.

Took a few more shots. Imagined Robertson guarding me, hands up, arms wide.

You shutting me down, Miles? You think? Think again, man.

I hit a long jumper. The ball banged off the garage and rolled toward the street.

I tracked it down. Glanced over at Marcus's house. Saw his face in the window, grinning at me.

A few seconds later he was in the driveway.

Marcus knows me well enough not to say much in a situation like this. I shot the ball. He rebounded it. Tossed it back to me.

"Tomorrow," he said.

"You know it."

I shot again, and all I heard was net.

A very calming sound.

Marcus laughed. "I look out my window and there you are. Figured you'd be sound asleep, dreaming about the game."

"Too wound up," I said. "You know how I am."

"Do I ever." He turned and shot the ball. I ran in and grabbed it as it slipped through the net.

"Okay," he said. "Here we go."

I dribbled a few times, then drove to the hoop. Marcus slapped at the ball. I put both hands on it and leaped to shoot. The ball grazed the rim and fell.

Marcus boxed me out and grabbed the rebound, sprinting back past the free-throw line.

I guarded him tight. His moves had improved. He missed the shot, but he was back in my face as I dribbled away.

Five minutes of that. Playing hard and laughing. Then the spotlight went on and off a couple of times.

We stopped short. Dad opened the back door. "You're disturbing the peace," he said.

Marcus stopped dribbling. "Evening, Mr. Santana," he said with an embarrassed smile.

"Evening, Marcus." Dad jutted his thumb toward the door. "Torry."

"Got it," I said.

Marcus handed me the ball.

"Thanks," I said.

"Feel better?"

"Much."

"Let's do it again sometime." Marcus laughed as he walked down the driveway.

Now I knew I could handle it. The presentation and the game. I might even get some sleep.

I was ready for Robertson. I wondered if he was ready for me.

97

TEN

Not Fooled

Deep breath, Torry. No pressure.

I pointed to my poster and explained to the class that the solar system hides many places that could have life.

"Who knows what it might look like?" I said. "But there are creatures in the most remote, coldest, driest, wettest, and hottest places on Earth. So scientists believe life can thrive almost anywhere."

Mrs. Lewis wanted to know how there could be liquid water on planets so far from the sun. That was easy. Then she asked if there would be enough oxygen out there.

"Maybe the creatures breathe some other substance," I replied. "No one knows yet. I hope to be the one who finds out. I want to do science as my real job someday."

"Excellent work, Torry," she said. "Does anyone else have questions?"

Griffin raised his hand. He had a giant grin, so I knew he was going to bust me. "Where do flying saucers come from?" he asked.

"Careful, I think they fall out of cabinets," I said.

Javon was next. "Why does Saturn have rings?"

"It's engaged to Jupiter."

Mrs. Lewis laughed. I'm pretty sure I aced the presentation.

One hurdle down.

I took another big breath.

Bring on Miles Robertson.

When our bus pulled into the parking lot behind Central Middle School, I finally looked up. I'd been staring at the back of the seat in front of me for the entire ride, trying to breathe normally and stop my heart from racing.

Trust your instincts, I kept thinking. Don't overreact to Robertson's fakes.

Marcus had given up trying to talk to me. He'd moved a few rows back and sat with Javon and Griffin. All of the eighth graders were farther back, so I was the first player off the bus.

And the first person I saw was Robertson.

He stood outside the gym, wearing his warm-up suit and talking to a couple of adults. He looked calm like he always did, but he was eyeing the bus.

It was no accident he was out there. He was smart enough to know he's intimidating. His team hadn't lost a game in more than a year, and he was a big part of that. He wanted us to see right away who we'd be up against, as if we'd forgotten.

Robertson was averaging twenty-three points a game—almost double the next-highest scorer in the league.

We made eye contact as I walked by. He gave me a little smile and lifted his eyebrows. I just nodded.

I knew he was trying to psych me out.

I didn't have to outplay him—I just needed to play better than last time. He'd outscored me by eighteen points, but we'd only lost by seven. And it could have been much closer than that.

Central's gym is bigger and newer than ours, with a shiny, polished floor. The bleachers were full. I looked around for my dad and saw him next to Marcus's dad in the top row. They'd closed the office early to see this.

I'd been waiting two weeks for this game. Some nights I'd dreaded it; other nights I couldn't wait.

Now it was here.

During the warm-up drills, I kept sneaking looks down the other end of the court. Robertson looked confident. He deserved to be.

I had everything else tuned out. Hadn't said a word since lunchtime. Felt a little hollow. A lot nervous. Central was undefeated, but we were 7–1. We'd be tied for first if we could pull this one off.

"Wake up," Marcus whispered. "This is it."

I gave my head a shake. "Right."

We took the court. I shook Robertson's hand and stepped behind him.

The crowd made more noise than any I'd ever played in front of, and they never quieted down. We hustled like crazy, but we were off our game. Central went up 2–0, then 4–0, then 7–0 before Mitchell made a lay-up.

I'd usually sprint back on defense, but something made me stay. Robertson took the inbounds pass and casually turned. It wasn't like him to be careless, and I swatted the ball from his hand. Before he could react, I'd driven to the hoop and scored.

This time I sprinted back to my teammates.

Robertson looked a little less calm for a change. He brought the ball up quickly and made a hard drive toward the hoop. He got past me, but I forced him out of the lane. He took an off-balance shot, and it barely grazed the rim.

Who's overreacting now?

Mitchell grabbed the rebound, and we were off. Barnes's jumper closed the lead to a single point, and the Central coach called time-out. We'd changed the momentum in a hurry.

I don't think either team led by more than two points for the rest of the first half. Robertson scored his share, but he wasn't burning me as often as last time. I was racking up assists and managed another steal.

We headed to the locker room down 24–23. Pretty good work.

When I saw Dugan, it dawned on me that I'd played every minute. I'd just stayed focused. Never even thought I needed a rest.

It had been a physical first half. Barnes and Mitchell had three fouls apiece, but Coach said he had no intention of sitting them.

I led the way back to the court.

"Same five," Coach said as we huddled. "No dumb fouls. But don't back down."

I felt completely different than I had before the game. No more nerves. I couldn't wait for the second half. Couldn't care less what the stats were.

I looked up at my dad. He patted his shirt. I nodded. Watch his waist.

Robertson opened the half with a three-pointer, but we clawed back and tied it up. Back and forth we went, neither team building a lead. Everything seemed cool until Barnes got called for a reach-in foul with a minute left in the quarter.

Coach yanked him out. Marcus came in.

We were all tired, but that's better than being cold. I needed to work Marcus gradually into the flow. When we regained possession, I threw him the ball, but called for it right back. He needed a few safe touches.

We held for the final shot of the quarter, working the ball around the perimeter. With seconds left, I passed to Marcus. Robertson drifted over to him, and for a second I was open.

Marcus passed me the ball. I launched a three-pointer from the top of the key.

Swish. Nothin' but net.

We ran to the bench with a one-point lead.

Barnes reported back in. The next several minutes were frantic. Sprinting, dodging, backpedaling, driving. Mitchell dominated inside, hauling down rebounds and banking in lay-ups. The pace was incredibly fast.

When Mitchell got fouled, I stood outside the key with my hands on my knees, panting from chasing Robertson. For once I was glad when Dugan reported in. Barnes came back in, too.

I walked to the bench. "Catch your breath," Coach said. "You'll be right back in."

The clock said 2:17. Score tied, forty-six apiece. Long way to go.

Mitchell made the first free throw. The second bounced off the back of the rim and fell to the side. Barnes leaped for it, reaching over the shoulder of the Central center.

Tweet. Another foul.

Barnes's fifth. He was done.

"Torry," Coach said firmly. I hurried to the scorer's table.

There was 2:14 left. I'd officially been out of the game for three seconds.

I looked at Coach. "Point guard," he said. He made sure Dugan heard it.

Dugan and I were never on the court at the same time. Marcus was usually Barnes's backup, but Coach didn't make that switch. He wanted Dugan to play the other guard position, and that made sense to me. Dugan's experience was worth more than Marcus's.

Robertson took his time bringing up the ball. He looked winded. This was going to come down to a two-minute frenzy, and he was setting that up. The people in the bleachers were going nuts.

I guarded him closely, not letting him drive. He kept darting and stepping back, waiting for me to overreact to a move.

Finally he passed the ball. He cut into the lane, yelling for it back, but I stuck to him. His teammate tried to force a pass anyway. The ball was mine.

Dugan sprinted toward our basket, wide open. I took two dribbles, got clear, made the long pass.

Easy lay-up.

First assist from me to Dugan. Ever.

Three-point lead.

And here came Robertson. I knew that look. Fierce and determined. He was taking this game into his own hands.

That's when a guy can overreact.

I forced him outside, made him dribble toward the corner. He pivoted, swooped back to the top of the key, looking for an open shot. I stayed glued to him.

"Screen!" Dugan yelled, but it was too late. I banged hard into Central's other guard. Robertson sliced past, went up to shoot.

Mitchell blocked the shot!

This time I was free. Dugan picked up the loose ball and fired the same pass I'd just done. I chased down the ball, dribbled twice, and laid it softly off the backboard.

Five-point lead! Less than a minute left. This was going to happen.

But Robertson didn't think so.

His eyes were narrow and his mouth was set in a sneer. I stayed on my toes as he dribbled in front of me. He drove left, took one step right, and leaned back as I tried to keep my balance.

The ball flew over my head in a perfect arc and fell cleanly through the net. Three points. Our lead was down to two.

Central pressed. Dugan had a hard time getting the ball in, and I ran side to side with Robertson all over me. Finally he made the pass. I dribbled fast up the court. Crossed the center line. Heard Coach calling to take a time-out.

The score was 49–51. Only up by two, and twenty-eight seconds left. An eternity.

"Eat the clock," Coach told us in the huddle. "No forced shots. They'll foul when they have to."

Dugan took the ball on the sideline. Robertson was in my face. I stepped upcourt, then sprinted way back and took the safe pass.

Everyone in the bleachers was on their feet. Robertson and the other guard swarmed me, but I shielded the ball and raced around them.

Pass to Dugan. Take it back. Elude them as long as you can.

Fouled.

We'd eaten up half the time. With just fourteen seconds left, I could all but seal this win. It was one-and-one. If I made the first free throw, I'd get a second. Make them both and it was all but over.

Dugan met my eye and shook his fist. "All you, Santana," he said. Good words. Another first.

I felt confident. Like I was shooting in my driveway. Alone. No pressure.

I let out my breath. Bounced the ball twice. Shot the ball the same way I'd done a million times.

It rolled around the rim. And fell out!

"Hustle!" somebody yelled.

I searched for Robertson. He had the ball.

One stop, I told myself. No way he scores.

Would he take it to the hoop and go for the tie? Or try to win the game with a three? My bet was that he'd go for the win right here. There was so much energy in the gym, so much excitement. He was a gamer. This was how he did it.

He juked left at the top of the key, then popped back. I made the same step, but kept my balance. Kept my eyes on his waist.

There it was. The telltale move. He lunged, then stepped back and elevated himself to shoot.

I hadn't been fooled. I reached as high as I ever had, and the ball slid over my fingertips. I made just enough contact with it. Just enough to alter its flight.

I turned and watched. The ball hit the front of the rim and skimmed harmlessly to the floor.

Thunk.

The buzzer sounded. Robertson shut his eyes. Somebody lifted me off my feet and every one of my teammates started yelling.

Me, too.

I bumped fists with Dugan and Mitchell. My teammates. I knew one thing for sure. Our team would be better than ever for the rest of the season.

111

"You're the man!" Marcus said. "This time, you schooled him."

I laughed. I hadn't schooled Robertson at all. He was the best player on the court. I hadn't shut him down, but I'd played a lot better than last time. Enough to stop that last shot.

Enough to win.